This igloo book belongs to:

....

igloobooks

Published in 2018
by Igloo Books Ltd
Cottage Farm
Sywell
NN6 0BJ
www.igloobooks.com

GOL002 0918
2 4 6 8 10 9 7 5 3 1
ISBN 978-1-78905-192-6

Written by Carrie Lewis
Illustrated by Martin Irish

Printed and manufactured in China

Little, Lost Penguin

igloobooks

An egg sat on the slippery ice, as cold as cold could be.
It perched alone, a tiny shape, down by the icy sea.

Then suddenly, the eggshell broke! Out came a tiny beak.
A penguin chick sat on the ice and gave a little squeak.

He shook his body, looked around and flapped his wings, too.
Feeling all alone, he whispered, "Mummy, where are you?"

A passing gull saw Little Chick and swooped down very low.
"That baby bird looks lost," he thought. "I'll stop to say hello."

"Little Chick," said the gull, "it's too cold to be outside.
You can shelter under my wing. It's a nice, warm place to hide."

"Can you help?" said Little Chick. "I can't find my mummy!
I'm all alone and very cold, do you know where she could be?"

"Of course I'll help you," squawked the gull. "Let's fly into the air. We'll be able to see lots of things from all the way up there."

"It's so much fun," said Little Chick, whizzing over the snow.
"Look! There are some silly seals, playing down below."

The seals got so excited, they clapped and yelled, "Hello! Would you like to play with us? It's fun. Come on, let's go!"

They had such a great time, slipping, sliding and wriggling.
"Weeeee!" cried Little Chick, flapping his wings and giggling.

Then Little Chick said, "Thank you both for asking me to play, but I still need to find my mummy. I must be on my way."

Suddenly, a spurt of water sprayed out of the sea.
A giant whale popped up and said, "You can ride along with me."

So, Little Chick held on to Whale, as the waves below went crash!
Then one big wave came along and he fell in with a splash!

"Glug, glug, glug," he went, floating past shimmery, shiny fish.
Following them he flicked his tail and moved his wings with a swish.

Swimming faster and faster and flapping more and more,
soon Little Chick shot right out of the water and back onto the shore.

Looking like a soggy ball of fluff, his fur went drip, drip, drip.
Whale, the seals and the gull laughed, saying, "You've had quite a trip."

Suddenly, Little Chick cried, "Look!" pointing with one of his wings.
"I see a crowd of purple and white, waddling, cheeping things!"

He tripped and slipped and skidded, but he didn't seem to care.
Running through the ice and snow, soon he was almost there.

When Little Chick reached the crowd they pressed around so near.
A smiling penguin said, "At last. I'll tell our mum you're here."

"Mum was looking after you. She watched your egg all day.
Then a great big storm came up and your egg rolled away."

So, at long last Little Chick had found his family huddle,
But best of all he found his Mummy and had a big, warm CUDDLE!